M000040685

The Great Game

The Way to Freedom

Book 9

H.M. Clarke

Sentinel Publishing

Also by H.M. Clarke

The Order
1: Winter's Magic
Marion: An 'Order' Short Story

John McCall Mysteries
1: Howling Vengeance

The Great Game

The Way to Freedom

Book 9

H.M. Clarke

Sentinel Publishing

Copyright © H. M. Clarke 2018

All rights reserved; no part of this publication may be reproduced or transmitted by any means, electronic, mechanical, photocopying or otherwise, without the prior permission of the copyright owner.

First published in The United States of America in 2018

Sentinel Publishing, Dayton, Ohio.

Cover design by Deranged Doctor Design

The moral rights of the author have been asserted.

DEDICATION

As always, this book is dedicated to my two beautiful
children, Keith and Ariadne.

CONTENTS

"Don't trust yourself until the day you die."

-A Saying of the Suenese

CHAPTER ONE

Fort Foxtern was in turmoil.

And Captain Jerant, as the nominal commander did nothing to still it. Colonel Oded was furious and had sent numerous letters off to Hered in an effort to hurry the issue of the order to select the head of the Northern Army. It should have been given to Prince Garrick straight off, but for some unknown reason, the Emperor was delaying the appointment.

Oded and Harada had a very good idea as to what might be the reason for that delay.

The Emperor's Mistress. Felian.

She and her cronies were undoubtedly working to turn this conflict into something that they can use to their advantage.

It also did not help matters that the returning scouts had reported large numbers of men massing along the Arranian side of the border and that signs of passing Arranian groups had been seen in the forests and mountains around them.

It was early morning and Harada and Oded stood on the large open plain before the main gates of Fort Foxtern. Red Samar stood with them, her large form blocking the two men from view from any unfriendly eyes looking on them from the fort. Around them mustered the rest of the Wing. Hatar'le'margarten stood patiently as their riders placed the lightweight riding tack over their shoulders and made sure that the harness and straps were secure.

"We should have heard something back by now," Harada quietly said as he adjusted the girth strap on Samar's double saddle.

"I know. But the decision cannot be delayed for too much longer," Oded replied standing back a few steps as Harada flung the neck strap around Samar.

"I was talking about Garrick. He should have sent us news about what he's seen going on at the Capital. He or Malchance must have some idea

5

of what exactly She is doing or saying to delay the announcement."

"It may be unsafe for him to send messengers Harada. He and his movements will undoubtedly be watched and reported back to Her."

Harada stood up and began to make a show of adjusting Samar's chest strap.

"I know. But Garrick's a resourceful fellow. He would work out a way to get word to us." Under his breath, he muttered, "I want to know how he feels about Kalena being missing." Harada leaned his head against Samar's broad chest and he soaked up her silent strength as he tried to still his whirling thoughts. All of Garrick's plans hinged around that girl. Harada's niece had better come back to them safe and sound. A blast of air on the back of his head caused him to smile as a moment later he felt the reassuring touch of a feathered nose just above his ear.

Harada stood back from Samar and then reached up to give her a scratch under her chin.

"I just hope he is still safe. I don't trust Felian as far as I can throw her."

Oded nodded and looked over his shoulder at the great arm of the Bhaligier ranges. Harada followed his gaze until his eyes alighted on the towering peak of Daegourouf. Unlike the rest of the ranges, the skirts of the mountain did not hold snow. Only its utmost peak had a small cap of white that made it blend into the clouds behind it. This made the mountain stand out amongst its fellows.

"The scouts came back in last night, and after reporting to Jerant and Inman, the lead scout

7

came to report to me."

"Jerant still is not sharing information with you?"

Oded smiled, his white teeth bright against his dark olive skin. "He shares what he thinks I won't be interested in. But most of the men here know that command will eventually be given to Prince Garrick and so to me. They know which side to butter their bread."

Harada pulled his eyes away from the mountain. "And just what did the scout have to say?"

"They have not seen any sign of Ice Tiger activity around the immediate area of Foxtern. They have seen signs of Arranian troops moving through, but the enemy was long gone before the scouts saw their signs. The only troop movements they have seen with their own eyes is that of Jerant's men who the scout says looks to be following the trail of the Arranians."

"Jerant's men following the Arranians? Don't tell me he's actually doing something sensible and is keeping an eye on the enemy," Harada said.

Oded shook his head. "I don't know. The Infantry scout didn't say as much, but I get the impression that the man did not like what he saw."

Harada's shrewd gaze centered on Oded who was now looking intently at him.

"Are you inferring that Jerant has something to do with the Arranians?"

Oded shrugged.

"I'm not inferring anything. At least not without hard proof."

9

Harada released the breath he had been holding. "If he is really in league with the enemy, it would mean a death sentence for him."

"And it couldn't happen to a nicer man."

'Harada, men are coming through the gate.'

Samar's warning made Harada turn to see a small group of Jerant's cronies walking slowly out from the main gate towards the flying field. Undoubtedly coming to spy on them.

'Samar, pass a message on to Holm through Motta. Tell them to do a high attitude search for any signs of either Jerant's men, or the Arranians that the scout group had seen signs of. If he sees them, he is to observe to see what their interactions are. Any signs of collusion between the two groups and Holm is to report back to either Me

or Colonel Oded.'

'Yes, Harada.' After a pause. *'Holm and Motta acknowledge the order and they are on their way.'*

Looking over Samar's shoulder, Harada saw Holm mount Motta and the two quickly launched into the clear morning sky and flew off towards the main arch of the Bhaligers and Daegourouf.

"Oded, we have company coming in our direction," Harada said.

The Colonel turned and looked towards the gate. "I see Jerant is sending his eyes out."

"I'd say it was Inman who has. Jerant prefers not to think about us so much." Harada let a smile tug at his lips. "It doesn't matter though, I've lived my life under the gaze of the Justicars."

"They only have the authority they currently have because of Felian. If they didn't need her, the Justicars would hang her to the wind."

Harada tightened his lips but said nothing in reply. He and Garrick should have moved quicker to stop Felian from gaining the foothold she currently has. The current situation is as much their fault as hers.

"We'd better move the wing out otherwise they will wonder why we are waiting." Harada turned away from the gate and in one swift movement swung himself up into the first seat of Samar's double saddle. He deftly tied the security straps before leaning down to give Oded a hand to mount behind him.

Upon seeing their Wing Commander mount, the rest of the wing did themselves and then waited for the signal to fly.

Once Oded had secured his straps, Harada and Samar checked the readiness of the wing. Everyone was mounted and waiting. Harada noted that the group of cronies was still walking towards the Flying Field. He waited until the first man was about to set foot past the white washed rocks that bordered the Flying Field. He and Samar then gave the order.

'Rise.'

As one, the entire wing leaped from the field, leaving the ground below swirling in sand and wind from the powerful down beats of the launching Hatar'le'margarten.

Harada saw the group of men rock back in surprise and begin to cough and splutter before using their coats to protect their faces from the stinging dust and wind.

It was a childish thing to do, but it gave Harada a perverse satisfaction. Any act of resistance no matter how small was good for a person's soul.

He felt Oded grab the back of his jacket as Samar ascended at a steep rise to reach patrol attitude. The Colonel hated to fly, but this was the only space they had where they could be sure not to be overheard.

After what seemed an age but would only have been a dozen heart beats at most, Samar began to level out and around them, Harada watched as the rest of the wing slipped into standard diamond formations.

"We are going to have to come up with a story about why Wing Second's Tayme and Trar and Adhamh are missing. Jerant seems to have a special interest in them, and would love to have a reason to mark them as deserters."

"It's none of his business where they are. The Flyers are placed under my command. If I say they are out on official business then that should be enough for Jerant."

Oded eased the hold on Harada's jacket as he talked. The morning was a good one for flying. A pristine blue sky, high altitude wind currents strong enough to give the Hatar lift to help them conserve energy, but light enough not to buffet the riders strapped to their necks. The air Harada breathed still held a hint of winter and the day already felt good.

"Jerant might still try something. Or maybe stir Inman up to look into it. As I said, Jerant has a

15

special interest in those three, especially Kral Tayme. He and Kalena are the two who he blames for his removal out here."

"Brock should have worked harder to have had him discharged from the service. It might have saved us the headache we have now."

Harada shrugged but gave no reply. He was loyal to the Provost Marshall and did not like to hear him criticized, even by someone else whom he respected.

The flight was now soaring over the skirts of the mountain range and Harada asked Samar to give the order for the flight to follow them along the border down the Suenese side of the Ranges.

Samar banked in a leisurely turn and then settled in the new direction.

Oded leaned forward a little to look down

past Samar's shoulder. "How can you see anything from up here? The forest down below just looks like green dyed wool."

"The Hatar can see what lies below. As you very well know. They have very sharp eyes, but even they will miss something if they are not looking in the right direction."

A rumble from Samar drew a chuckle from Harada. "Samar says that she has never been caught by surprise."

'Except when you are asleep in a sand bath in the sun.'

'I knew that was you, Harada!'

'Sure you did.'

'I didn't eat you did I?'

Harada chuckled again and thumped Samar companionably on her neck.

'No. You didn't and I am very thankful.'

"How long are we going to patrol for?" Oded asked.

"About six hours is standard. So we'll be back at Foxtern about mid afternoon. If we come back earlier it might look suspicious."

"So that means I'll be eating lunch on Hatar back again then."

"Yes, it does."

"Figures." The Colonel then settled back in the saddle for a long trip.

CHAPTER TWO

"Harada, what's that?" Oded pointed down to the forest ahead of them.

Harada was already looking at the location, but as yet could not discern anything. Samar had alerted him that there were a group of men down there heading along the path in the direction of Fort Foxtern. Oded must have good eyes.

"The Hatar have already seen it Oded," Harada called back over his shoulder. "There is a group of men on the road and until they can be directly sighted, we can't be sure if they are ours or not."

"Are we going to go down and check?" Oded asked.

"No need, there is a gap in the trees not far ahead of them along the road they follow, the Hatar will see who they are then."

Even though Harada could not see him, the Wing Commander could tell that the colonel was not happy about waiting. He was a man of action and sitting still when the enemy may be below them did not sit well with the man.

"They may be Pydarki as well-"

'Harada, Motta is coming in ahead of us,' Samar's mind speak cut into Harada's words.

'Motta?'

'Yes, she says that she and Holm have some interesting news for us.'

'Interesting? Is that all she said?'

'Yes.'

"What is wrong Harada?" Oded asked, placing a hand on Harada's shoulder to get his attention.

"Hold on a moment," Harada muttered and pointed by way of explanation ahead of him. He could now see the blue form of Motta flying towards them.

'Samar, ask Motta to report. Is there something we need to know about those men

21

beneath us?'

After what seemed a very long moment, Samar began to relay Motta's words.

'The group below are ours. They are under the command of Captain Vosloo. Lieutenant Peana had sent them back to report directly to Colonel Oded. But they did give us some other news. Kral and Peana have found Kalena!'

'They've found her? Where is she? Is she with the group below?'

'Holm wants to talk to you in person Harada.'

'I bet he does. That gap in the trees below near the road looks big enough for two Hatar to land. Tell Holm and Motta to meet us there.'

'Yes, Harada.'

"Oded, we may have some good news for a

change. Holm and Motta are ahead of us and they say that Kalena has been found."

"She has?" The Colonel's voice sounded both excited and relieved.

"The group below us are Captain Vosloo's men. They have been sent back to report directly to you. I am going to land below so that I can talk with Holm, the group on foot should reach us there and you can take their report."

"Thank the One we came across them before they came under the eyes of those at Fort Foxtern," Colonel Oded said. "Though I have a feeling this will be news that Prince Garrick will not be pleased with."

"You can count on it."

Harada saw Motta begin to descend to the clearing below and he gave the command to Samar to have her land to meet him. He gave orders for the rest of the wing to stay in a holding pattern over their location and to keep an eye out for any unfriendly folk that might be around.

Samar slowed her descent and landed daintily on her feet in the clearing not far from Motta. Holm was already descending from the blue Hatar's shoulder and before Samar had settled, both Harada and Oded were already unbuckling their security Straps. Holm stayed back until Samar had tucked in her wings and her riders had dismounted.

"Holm, what news?" Harada called, waving the flyer towards him. Oded rushed to the road to await the company of men.

"Wing Commander Harada, you'll hear this first hand from Vosloo's men. They have found Kalena, except that she doesn't know she's Kalena.

24

She thinks she's someone else. And she has an Ice Tiger brother. Oh! And she is now the Queen of the Ice Tigers."

"Wait, What?" Harada could not help the frown that washed over his face as Holm's words rushed over him.

Holm stopped and drew a deep breath as if to calm himself. But Harada could see the restrained excitement held at bay in Holm's taunt frame.

"Kalena is found but does not remember who she is," Holm started again though slower this time. "She was found by the Ice Tigers who took her in and gave her another name, which I can't remember at the moment. Anyway, something happened and Kalena became the new leader of the Ice Tigers. And now the Ice Tigers and the

Arranians are going to war with each other."

"The Arranians are fighting with the Ice Tigers?" Harada looked at Samar who just tilted her head in that annoying way that the Hatar'le'margarten had when they did not want to admit that they did not know.

'Motta confirms Holm's words. We'll hear the same from the group coming down the road towards us.'

"Wing Commander, do you have anything to eat? I'm starving."

Harada tried to hide his smile as he slipped a hand into his belt pouch and pulled out a wrapped wad of jerky.

"Here, this should take the edge off." Harada tossed him the food.

Holm deftly snatched the packet from the

air and quickly unwrapped it.

"Thanks, Wing Commander," he mumbled before tearing into the jerky.

"Holm, did the men say why Kalena, Kral and the two Hatar aren't with them?"

The Flyer nodded and quickly swallowed the food in his mouth.

"Yes. They, along with Lieutenant Peana and some of his men have gone to Daegarouf to talk to the Pydarki. I also forgot to say that Captain Vosloo was missing, the Lieutenant is looking for him."

"Vosloo's missing? So, we find one and then lose another. Oded is not going to be happy about this."

"Well, he's not missing anymore. This group of men has found him. The Captain is

27

traveling down the road with them."

Harada shook his head and Samar let out a rumble from her chest as if she was laughing.

"Holm, you really need to work on your reporting style."

Holm Lunman just nodded as he had gone back to gnawing on his piece of jerky.

'Motta says that Captain Vosloo will give a report to Oded, but the information on Kalena will need to be gleaned from the men. Vosloo was away while Kalena was with them.'

'What do you think about the news that Kalena is the Queen of the Ice Tigers?'

'Motta confirms that that is what the men had told Holm. The Ice Tigers look to Kalena as their leader and that the Ice Tigers are going to war with the Arranians. The Tigers blame them for a lot

of the killing that has happened to their people.'

'They do? We've killed Ice Tigers as well, does that mean they will come against us as well?' Harada mused.

'Maybe, or the Ice Tigers could just think that the Arranians are responsible for all of their deaths.'

Harada could hear the noise and then low voices through the underbrush from the direction of the path. The group of men had met up with Colonel Oded on the trail. He leaned back against Samar's shoulder to wait while the two Hatar talked privately among themselves. Holm moved to lean next to Harada, giving Samar a hard scratch around her wing join by way of compensation. It was a place that was an inconvenient spot to put a head or claw to so Samar did not mind.

Without saying a word, Harada plucked another packet of wrapped jerky from his pouch and handed it to Holm. Holm took it and eagerly tore the wrappings from it.

The sun had visibly moved a whole finger's width across the sky before the sounds of moving bodies came towards them. Harada and Holm pushed themselves away from Samar's side with Holm quickly brushing away jerky crumbs from his jacket front to make himself presentable.

Slowly, Harada saw men leading horses coming towards them. At their head, he recognized Captain Vosloo and Oded.

As Oded and Vosloo entered the clearing, the Coloenl gestured for Harada to move with them to one side, out of direct hearing of the main group.

Once the three of them were sure of their

privacy, Oded turned to Harada.

"We've caught them this time. We've got them. Inman is a dead man."

Harada's eyes widened at Oded's blunt words and his eyes flicked to Vosloo to gauge his reaction. The man showed no surprise.

"What do you mean?" he asked.

"Tell him, Frazier."

The Captain drew a deep breath, uncomfortable about something, but nothing related to this news.

"My men and I have discovered that there are some traitors lurking in the Suene Empire. We have witnessed with our own eyes Justicars meeting with Arranians along one of the Northern passes. My men have uncovered that there is a rogue Arranian group working on traitorous actions to their own country and that this is the group working with the Justicars. Prince Garrick and the Emperor need to know this."

"Do you have any physical proof of this treachery?" Harada asked.

"My Sergeant is carrying a packet captured from one of the rogue Arranians, and some of my men recognized some of the Justicars at the meeting as coming from Fort Foxtern. One of them was Videan Tsarland."

Harada's eyebrows shot up in surprise. That was the last name he expected to hear.

"Harada, we need to send word back to Garrick immediately. He needs to get ready for this so that he can stop things from progressing to outright war," Colonel Oded hissed.

Harada thought a moment and then decided.

"I'll send Holm and Motta with the news and the packet with orders to report only to Prince Garrick."

Oded nodded. "We'll return to Fort Foxtern with Captain Vosloo, who will report to me and Inman that the Arranians are massing only because of the Ice Tigers and not us. Make no mention of treachery until we hear back from Garrick. I want to see what his reaction is."

Oded turned to Vosloo. "Then, once we get a moment to ourselves, you can report to me the reason you left your men in the first place."

CHAPTER THREE

"You believe men not skilled in spy work when they tell you that the Arranians and the Ice Tigers are not Allied?"

Harada watched as Justicar Inman stopped his pacing to address both Colonel Oded and Captain Vosloo. Harada stood back by the door, an insect beneath the notice of the Justicar. Captain Jerant sat down in a chair behind Inman's desk, just as beneath the Justicar's notice as he was.

"I believe what they tell me they saw with their own eyes," Vosloo snapped back.

Even from his position, Harada could tell from Vosloo's tone and stance that he would prefer to be reporting to the man who on paper is supposed to be in command for Fort Foxtern. Not a Justicar.

"The camp of Ice Tiger dead? Done a few days ago?" the Justicar snorted. "That work was not done by the Arranians. That nest had been cleared out by Jerant's men."

"What?" Oded could not keep the surprise from his voice, as he turned to look at Vosloo.

"They killed a group of Arranians in retaliation. Why would they do that if they were allies?"

Inman shrugged. "How would I know what goes through the mind of a beast."

Harada noted that Jerant moved uneasily in his chair, but made no effort to speak. Inman was making sure that all knew who was really in charge here.

"Our intelligence states that the Arranians are massing to attack us and that they have an Alliance with the Ice Tigers. We will keep our troops ready to act against any form of Arranian or Ice Tiger aggression.

Harada gritted his teeth. His father should have officially announced Garrick's control of the armies by now. The fact that he hasn't as yet must be due to Felian's work. Harada fervently hoped that his brother was making headway in cutting her

37

down.

"If the Arranians were going to attack us, wouldn't they have done it already? Now would be the perfect time since only a small part of the army is stationed in the pass. Their forces could punch an entry here with ease and minimal losses."

Inman scowled, and then resumed his pacing. The man was agitated. And annoyed. He was not happy about being questioned and contradicted.

"When Prince Garrick takes control of the Northern Armies, he will not look favorably on those who did not prepare adequately."

Colonel Oded made the implied warning implicit in his words. Harada could tell that the man was frustrated, but bringing Garrick's name into this atmosphere could only make matters worse.

Inman paused in his pacing, one foot balanced on his heel, hesitating on completing its step. If Harada didn't know any better, he would think that Inman felt fear. Strange that even the mention of his brother's name would cause that reaction. Maybe Felian and her cronies are not as secure in their position than they first thought. Father must still be loyal and listening to his son.

Then an unnerving thought entered Harada's mind. Maybe the reason Garrick's command had not yet been announced is that their father wanted to keep him in the Capital. Maybe their father was not as under Felian's control as they thought. Maybe...Maybe's are cloud dreams. Not real until they happen.

The Justicar's foot abruptly fell to the

ground and the man continued his pacing. The scowl that crossed the man's pale face showed plainly his annoyance to his reaction to Oded's words. But the man gave no answer to the Colonel.

"Captain Jerant and I will only act upon intelligence gathered from reliable sources."

"Are you inferring that my men are not reliable?" Vosloo's voice was not raised, but the threat in it was unmistakable.

"I am inferring that they are not trained to know what they are seeing."

Oded placed a warning hand on the Captain's shoulder and the retort that was boiling on his lips was swallowed back like bile.

"Until we have this information verified by our own intelligence agents, we will continue to operate as if the Arranians are planning on attacking us. You are dismissed."

Harada bristled at the casual dismissal of the Colonel as if he were a common infantryman, but the Colonel said nothing. He grabbed Vosloo by the upper arm and they both turned and left the room. Harada fell into step just behind them and closed the door as they exited.

No one spoke a word as they walked past the fort buildings back to the army encampment that skirted around the rear of the fort. As soon as they arrived back by their tents and campfire, Vosloo exploded.

"What in The One's name just happened?"

Oded raised his hands. "Not so loud Frazer," he hissed. "Even here there may be unwelcome ears listening in."

Vosloo visibly took control of himself

though Harada could see that his fisted hands were held tightly at his sides.

"What just happened was a confirmation that what you witnessed in the pass is connected to the Justicars here at Fort Foxtern," Harada's voice sat low in his throat.

"So, the traitors ARE working with the Arranians."

"So it seems."

Oded sat down on one of the large logs arranged in a circle around the fire. Harada followed suit and, after a moment's hesitation, so did Vosloo.

"I hope Holm doesn't have any trouble finding Garrick. Felian's feelers might be more extensive than we thought," Oded muttered.

"Holm can be quite resourceful when he

wants to be," Harada answered. "And Inman gave me the impression that Felian's power might not be as strong as we thought."

Oded cocked his head and gave Harada a quizzical look. "What do you mean?"

"I don't think their control over Father is as absolute as they would like it to be. I think that the reason Father hasn't made Garrick overall commander is that he wants Garrick close to him."

"You got all that from Inman's pacing?" Vosloo's disbelief was plain in his voice.

"And from what he didn't say," Harada finished with a small smile.

"Either way. It still doesn't diminish the danger we are in at the moment. It seems that the Justicars here want us to go to war with Arran," Oded said.

"And the Ice Tigers want to go to war with Arran as well," Vosloo said slowly as if thinking on the issue.

"And the Arranians are going to war with the Ice Tigers. Not us."

"Unless something is done to provoke them." Harada shot up from his seat.

"Vosloo, do you think that was what that meeting in the pass was about? Arranging a confrontation to start a war?"

Frazier Vosloo started to nod. "It makes sense. Our rogue Justicars and those Arranians are wanting to stir a fight between everyone."

"So, why did you take off from your men?" Oded suddenly asked.

Harada sat back down on his log as Vosloo started to reply.

"Our camp was attacked by something. At first, I thought it was Ice Tigers but it turned out to be something quite different."

"Different? What do you mean?"

"Let's just say that there is more in these mountains to worry about than just the Ice Tigers. It looked like a giant demon hound and it's saliva ate everything it touched. One tried to get into the tent of my Lieutenant... I decided that I would track this thing myself. Don't ask me why I did that. At the time it seemed like the right thing to do, and for some reason, I felt this animal was somehow linked to the Pydarki, just as I think the Pydarki are involved with Kalena's disappearance."

Harada jerked back in surprise, not quite believing what he had just heard from Vosloo's lips. He saw the look of startled surprise come over

Oded's face as well.

"What makes you think the Pydarki have anything to do with this? It was more likely an Arranian Spellcrafter. Except that the Ice Tigers somehow got to Kalena first before the Arranians could."

Oded quickly recovered himself. "Yes. Holm told us that the Ice Tigers are no friends to Arran, that they are fighting each other in the mountains. I still cannot believe that Kalena is now their leader…"

"But as their leader, the Ice Tigers will not be attacking us. I notice that you did not report that to Inman."

Harada leaned forward, resting his elbows on his knees, waiting for Oded to respond.

"No. I didn't. But it will be reported to

Prince Garrick."

"Do you believe that if you had reported to the Justicar that the Ice Tigers were now being led by a Hatar Kalar that he would have sent men out to actively kill any Ice Tigers they found?"

Oded nodded. "He would do it in an effort to kill Kalena. He can't have a fly in the ointment spoiling their plans."

"Just as he is the fly in our ointment spoiling ours?" Vosloo said drawing both men's attention back to himself.

Oded looked back at him but said nothing.

"Did you end up finding your monster, Frazier?" Harada asked to cut the stilted silence.

"No. I saw no sign of it once I lost that initial trail, but I swear I could feel them watching me."

Harada raised an eyebrow at the vehement emotion in Vosloo's voice.

"That thing came into our camp looking for something. Or someone. I want to know why."

"Instead of finding your monster dog, you found a small group of your men," Harada said, trying to get the conversation back on track.

"Yes. And we watched and listened to those traitors as they waited for their Arranian accomplices. Their talk as they waited incriminated them as surely as if we had seen them meet with the bastards themselves."

"Well, too bad they didn't incriminate Inman," Oded muttered.

"He's just as guilty and we all know it," Frazier spat out. "We should incarcerate him and all his cronies to meet the justice of the crown."

"Not without solid evidence we can't," Harada sat back and looked at both men. "This discussion is mute until we hear back from Garrick, or if Inman drags us into a war, not of our choosing."

Oded Sighed. "Let us hope Garrick is having more luck than we are in the Capital."

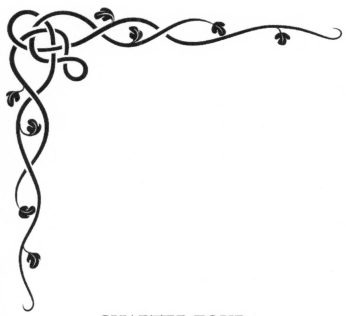

CHAPTER FOUR

Things were going well, so it shouldn't have

surprised Garrick when he encountered a little

friction when entering the Imperial city. The

soldiers being called up to join the Northern

Defense were encamped a mile from the Imperial

Capital's walls. It was orderly, respectful, even

with the usual camp followers, merchants and 'entertainment' providers attracted to the call of the easy coin.

Shatal snorted and shook his head causing Malchance's grey to nicker and bare his teeth.

"Now, now Shatal." Garrick slapped the horse affectionately on the neck. "You're a warhorse, remember. You need to get used to being dirty and mud splattered again."

Shatal just flattened his ears against his head and raised his nose so that it was above the dust of the road.

"I think Shatal has the right of it Garrick." Malchance moved in his saddle adjusting his weight while reining his grey back in to stop him nipping at the black. "I'd prefer to face a horde of Arranian blades than the viper's nest we are now heading into."

Prince Garrick gave the Duke a grim smile and glanced back over his shoulder. Behind them rode a full company of Garrick's elite guard. One hundred elite warriors dressed in their ceremonial best, banners streaming from their lances and completely devoted to the safety of their prince. The dust of the road did nothing to detract from the effect, and it will give a message to the citizens of Hered that the imperial family still holds power within its walls.

"The Honor Guard is a nice touch, Garrick. I know you don't like the ostentation but it is for the peoples benefit, not yours."

"I know Willard. I want Felian to get the message that I will not roll over and get my belly rubbed like my father. It takes a lot more than sweet words and seduction to bring me under her power, and that's all she dabbles in."

Malchance sneezed as the dust tickled his nose. "And she's tried both on you already."

"No one is going to replace Caitin in my bed or my heart. No one." Garrick's words smashed low and hard like granite rocks in the atmosphere around them.

"And I am not saying that you should Garrick, Caitin was my sister remember," Malchance replied in a hurry. "But the men will show Felian and her cronies that you mean to hold on to your Father's power and that you will not be unprotected."

"I know. By the One I hate Hered. I hate the politics, the sniping, the backstabbing, and the sycophancy... Harada should be in my place, he lives for this stuff."

Malchance let a small smile touch his lips. "But that is not the case and you will have to work with the hand fate has dealt you."

"I wish Harada were with me. I wish Kale-"

"Garrick!"

Garrick cut his words as Malchance's warning. He automatically looked about them, even knowing that there were no unwelcome ears around them. But the familiar pain rose up to overwhelm him, blanketing him in its sorrow.

"I just wish I didn't have to give her up."

"I know. I know. But you did it to protect her. Remember that first and foremost Garrick."

Garrick gave him a short nod of understanding. He looked along the road at the large imposing city gates. The Imperial City of Hered sat proudly among an elegant array of elder trees and manicured gardens. Built of the whitest stone that flashed blindingly whenever the rays of the sun crossed its gleaming towers of the Old City, it was once built for elegance and luxury. Over the ages that had slowly changed.

Defensive walls, gates, mazes, and death traps had been built around what was once, ornate outer walls and were so successful that the Old City had never been taken by force. The houses and trade districts of the New City were built around the old city like the open petals of a flower where most of Hered's population lived. Sometimes these newer additions blended so well with the old that it was now hard to tell where the old finished and the new began.

"I'm going to put things right Willard. I'm going to make sure that power and safety are placed back into our hands. Felian has remained too long unchecked and unchallenged."

"Garrick-"

"I can't believe father had let her have this much free rein. I. Am. Coming. To. Shut. Her. Down." The outburst was enough to clear the last of his pain and frustration out of his system.

"Feeling better now?"

"Much."

"Garrick, once we go through these gates, you cannot give in to these thoughts. You need to be strong and ruthless."

"I know and I will be. I know what the risk of failure will mean."

"Just keep that in mind. I favor keeping my

head attached to my neck, thank you very much."

Garrick knew he was supposed to laugh at the jest, but he could not bring himself to.

"There is something happening at the gate." Garrick gestured down the road where a large group of people had just started to stream out and line themselves up along the edge of the road. Malchance rose up in his stirrups to get a better look, and Garrick sent the Lieutenant of his Honor Guard down the road to find out what was going on. It was not long before the man was back. Captain Talon had moved up to ride on Garrick's other side, effectively boxing him in a protective cordon with Duke Malchance. Garrick sat straighter in his saddle, glad that he was not the only one finding the glittering mass of people lining up around the gate alarming.

"It might just be a welcoming party, Your Highness," Captain Talon's voice was low and not very reassuring,

"They've never given me one before. At least not one this large."

"And that is an awful lot of people there carrying sharp, pointy objects," Malchance said giving Garrick a grim smile.

"Killing the Crown Prince in front of the main gate of Hered is not a popular political move Willard." Garrick turned to his Captain.

"Captain Talon, tell the men to be alert."

"Yes, Your Highness," the Captain raised a hand and sent a signal back down the line to his men.

"It is probably just Felian wanting to show a guard presence larger than mine."

59

"It may be larger, Your Highness, but your own men are better trained. They are the elite of the army."

Garrick tried not to smile at the pride in Talon's voice. "That they are Talon. The fact that all my men always win the Guard's Tourney is as good a statement as anything that they are the best."

The smug look that crossed Talon's features improved Garrick's mood no end. It made him feel much better prepared to meet whatever unpleasantness awaited him ahead.

A dust cloud ahead told Garrick that his Lieutenant was returning and it was not long before his man's horse came skidding to a stop next to his Captain.

"Sir! A welcome party has been organized for Prince Garrick. It is being led by the Provost

Justicar."

"Ranen?" Then Malchance burst out laughing. "We must have spooked him good to have him come out into the daylight."

"Lieutenant, return to the line. Make sure that the men are presenting their best face for the spectators."

"Yes, Sir!" The man gave a quick salute to his Captain and reined his horse to go back down the line, issuing orders to the two sergeants.

"Talon, stay with us. I would like to hear your opinion later on your impressions."

"Yes, your highness."

"I can see his broodiness waiting right in front of the open gate." Malchance sat back into his saddle and held his reins loosely in one hand. "What do you want to do Garrick? Rush up towards

61

him or keep him waiting?"

"We keep the same pace, we don't want him thinking that his presence unnerves us. No sign of Felian then?"

"None."

"I give thanks to the One for small blessings."

"You won't be able to avoid her forever Garrick."

"I know, but I want to get a feel for what is happening in Hered and who I can still trust before I meet her again."

"She might not give you that wish."

"I'll deal with her when the time comes. Anyway, it's time to put on our smiles and our friendly façades."

"I don't do friendly," Garrick heard Talon

mutter but at least the man allowed the permanent frown on his face to soften a little.

"Try your best Captain."

A moment later, Garrick's company was just passing into the line of soldiers that bordered the road on either side of them. Ahead lay the main gates to the city towering above them all and now standing open. Before those open gates stood Provost Justicar Renan and a small group of his lackeys, all dressed in the thick black robes of the Book. Garrick noted that the guard lining the approach road was Imperial Guard. Since when does the Provost Justicar warrant being accompanied by Imperial Guard? Though the guard might only be here because of him, Garrick was hit with the distinct impression that this company of guards was used to operating under the Provost

Justicar's orders.

"Provost Justicar," Garrick said in way of greeting as he signaled Shatal to stop not a horse head away from the man. Talon and Malchance stopped half a horse length back on either side of him.

"Your Royal Highness." Ranen dropped into a low bow in greeting. "We welcome you back home to the Imperial Capital. Your Father sends his greetings."

"But is not here himself it seems," Garrick replied without emotion.

"His Imperial Majesty is recovering from his most recent illness and it was deemed too risky for him to come out to meet you."

The mention of his father's health bought that surge of anger rising back into Garrick's chest.

His father was as healthy as a horse. The man was being told constantly that he was old and frail, especially by a young, pretty woman who you thinks loves you, made him act like he was in his dotage.

Garrick fought the rage, and once he had it back under control, he let a small smile come to his lips. "Once we have settled and made ourselves presentable by removing the dust of the road, we will go and see our Father." Garrick made full use of the royal third person, using it to hammer home to all who heard that he was the Crown Prince and heir to the Imperial throne.

"Lady Felian requests your presence before you pay homage to His Imperial Majesty, Prince Garrick."

From the corner of his eye, Garrick saw

Malchance's head jerk up in surprise. Garrick let the smile fall from his lips. How dare she do this so openly.

"Felian can make arrangements with Duke Malchance if she wants to make an appointment to see me. If I have the time."

Garrick noted the lack of surprise that swept across Ranen's face at his response.

"Now. I am tired and in desperate need of a bath, and a nice meal."

The Provost Justicar stood in the middle of the road, clearly undecided at what to do. Felian's instructions obviously failed to cover him not wanting to follow Ranen to a meeting with her. Garrick waited a moment longer and when Ranen still did not move Garrick nudged Shatal forward, forcing the Provost Justicar to the side of the road to stand with the guard.

As he and his men entered the city, a large roar went up from the thousands of people lining the Emperor's Way to greet their Beloved Crown Prince.

"At least the people love you," Garrick heard Malchance say loudly over the din.

"For now at least, we'll see if they truly still love me after what I have planned comes to fruition.

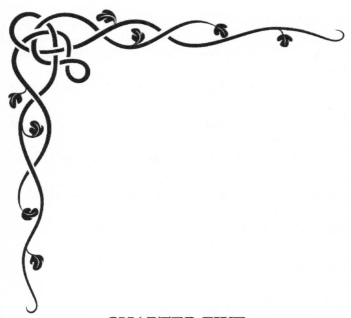

CHAPTER FIVE

Garrick slipped the clean shirt over his head and then used his fingers to tousle his still wet hair. He flopped onto the bed and quickly pulled on the clean pants that had laid out by one of the servants before his bath.

"Willard. You still out there?" Garrick

called out as he was pulling on his boots.

"….Yes." Malchance's response was not immediate and that made Garrick's head jerk up in concern. In one fluid motion, he stood up from the bed and scooped up the lounging robe that he had tossed onto a nearby divan and then threaded it around his body as he made his way to the bedroom door and flung it open.

"Willard-"

Garrick's words stuck in his throat as he caught sight of Malchance and the person standing with him.

"Prince Garrick, the Lady Felian to see you," Malchance said giving him a formal bow. Felian dipped into a deep curtsey, artfully showing the ample bosom popping out from her tightly laced bodice.

Garrick let his hand drop from the door and quickly folded the robe tightly around him and tying it securely shut. It was small enough protection against the serpent in the room, but the thick material of the robe would help turn a dagger if she had one.

"Felian," Garrick said by way of greeting.

Felian straightened and then took a few steps forward, completely ignoring Malchance as inconsequential.

"Your Highness. I am so glad to see you return to the Capital. Your father has been complaining that he does not see enough of you."

"We were getting ready to see him now. I take it you are arranging with Duke Malchance to make an appointment to see me?"

"Do I really need to make an appointment?"

she said moving forward again and running a finger gently up Garrick's arm. "Surely we can speak together as friends?" The finger moved to his shoulder and then slid slowly down his chest.

Garrick caught her hand and deliberately but forcefully moved it back to her. "You need to make an appointment Felian if you wish to speak seriously with me."

"Are you sure? I'm sure we can find a more enjoyable way to discuss our business."

Garrick gave her a grim smile. "I'm sure Felian. And considering how little effort you put into seducing me this time, you were sure of what my response would be."

Felian gave him one of her seductive smiles and tucked a lock of blonde hair that had escaped her immaculate coiffed looks back behind her ear.

The combination of silk and sheer material draped around her curves showing them to best effect. At first glance, she would draw the eye of most men. But on knowing her, Felian's appeal fails. Garrick's eyes were more drawn to Malchance who was standing behind her pulling a face.

"I still have to try darling. A handsome man like you just calls to be seduced. And I am not averse to mixing fun with business."

"I prefer to keep business separate Felian. And I have a policy of not sleeping with my father's women."

"Shame darling." Felian let the words linger in her mouth and then she turned and walked to the window. The light from which diffused through the sheer material and accentuated her body. The move might have worked on other men. But not Garrick.

"I am busy. Either make an appointment with Duke Malchance to see me later or I'll order my guard to escort you out."

"Testy. I'll go, just know this Garrick. It would be better for us both if we work together. You could have your army and power, all you have to do is work with me."

Garrick frowned and every muscle in his back stiffened.

"I am Garrick Thurad. Crown Prince of Suene and its imperial holdings. By law, I am first in line to my father and that is something that neither you nor he can ever change." Garrick's voice was low and deep and anyone who knew him would know that he was containing a focused anger. "Anyone who actively works against me is committing treason, and will be prosecuted to the utmost extent by the law."

From the corner of his eye, Garrick saw Malchance wince. He should not have made the threat, but something within Garrick moved him to say it.

"I only act for the defense of our country and way of life Garrick."

"Anyone who acts against the throne is committing treason Felian. Anyone."

"And your obsession with dismantling the Kalarthri and the Second Born Rule will pull our nation into chaos."

"Afraid that you will lose your state funded administrators Felian? You should be. Because once I am Emperor your source of imperial funding will be permanently dried up."

"You would do well to remember that you

are not Emperor yet."

"Are you making a threat to the Crown Prince?" Malchance said as he moved to place himself between Garrick and Felian.

"No darling, of course not," she said putting on her most sickeningly sweet smile. "Just making him aware that things can change. No one can predict the future."

Garrick watched as she flicked open her embroidered fan and began to fan herself

"I see you are busy. I will return later. Prince Garrick, Duke Malchance." Felian dropped into a small curtsey and then disappeared out of the receiving room.

Garrick waited until he could hear the outer door bang shut and his guard came to signal that Felian was gone.

"By the One, what was she doing here?" Garrick said once the guard had shut the door.

"She wouldn't have come here unless we, or something else, has her rattled. We must have her worried since she came herself instead of sending one of her flunkies."

"I can't stand the woman. What did she mean by saying I'm not Emperor yet? I know I'm not the emperor, and I hope not to be emperor for a long while yet. But I don't want my country in the hands of that woman, and father needs to take back control."

"We can discuss things with your father soon. But don't jump straight into the topic. You haven't seen your father in over a year, please make some small talk first."

"Very well Willard. I wasn't going too. I

can think for myself you know."

"Sorry Garrick," Malchance said raising his hands in a placating gesture. "I'm just nervous about what you'll find when you meet your father."

"It will be fine. Especially since this time I'm going to stay until Felian's power has been curtailed. I'm not going to take my father's word for it this time."

"What about the Northern threat? If your father gives you command of the Northern Army, then you'll have to go."

"I'll delegate command to Oded until I'm sure things are stable enough here in Hered."

Malchance glared at Garrick. "Are you sure that's a good idea? Her cronies might use that as an excuse to take power away from you."

"Let them try. Just let them."

CHAPTER SIX

The emperor's personal apartments were not far from Prince Garrick's suites. The prince now stood waiting in his father's receiving room along with Duke Malchance, Captain Talon and some of his select personal guard. The room was opulent and lush in bold reds and gold and it was still exactly the way Garrick remembered it from his childhood. The room had not been touched since his mother had last redecorated it. Garrick was glad that at least Felian had not got her claws into this. Father was not completely under her control.

The wait was not long.

The large double doors at the far end of the room opened and a clean faced freeman that Garrick did not recognize came through it.

"The Emperor is ready to see you now," the man said while sweeping down into a low bow.

Garrick gave the man a nod and then gave Malchance a meaningful glance. He then strode towards the door, Malchance fell in behind him and Captain Talon and his chosen men followed directly behind them.

The new room was large and spacious with a large fire roaring in the grate and plush arm chairs placed around it to get maximum warmth. Spaced around the walls were several footmen, waiting to jump to the Emperor's every whim. The tattoos on their cheeks showed them to be Kalarthri. But Garrick's eyes were drawn to the chair placed closest to the fire.

"Hello, my boy. Come, sit down."

Garrick's father patted the arm of the chair next to him as he talked and as he moved, the blanket covering him slipped to reveal old stains in the lounging robe he wore.

Garrick frowned but quickly sat in the chair offered by his father. Malchance and the others stayed where they stood. Protocol dictated that they had to remain standing in the Emperor's presence unless told otherwise. As he made himself comfortable in the chair, Garrick noted that his father's hair was unwashed and oily and his beard and mustaches had not been trimmed or cleaned.

"Hello father," he said. "How are you? Ranen said that you had been feeling ill."

"Phish," Groudin said waving away his son's concern with a weak wave of his hand. "I'm feeling fine. All these fusspots worrying about me falling ill. It's damned annoying."

"So, you haven't been sick?"

"Just a cold, nothing more. But I haven't seen you in a dog's age, Garrick. Catch me up on all the news."

"The news?"

"Yes, tell me all that has happened since you were last here."

Garrick was suddenly thrown into confusion. Surely his father would want to talk about the war? Garrick threw a look at Malchance who gave him an imperceptible shake of his head.

Garrick turned back to his father. "I've seen Harada. He's doing well."

"Harada! You need to tell him to come and see me. I can't remember the last time he came back home."

"Father. He is a Wing Commander, he can't leave his unit without his superior's permission."

"A prince does not need permission."

"But Harada is not a Prince. Not anymore. He is a Hatar Kalar."

Groudin's happy expression fell from his face, quickly replaced by one of concentration.

"He is Hatar Kalar. I forgot..."

His father's voice was low and was almost a whisper. He then shook himself and swung his gaze to the servants scattered around the room. "Leave us."

The voice was deep and commanding and after a moment of hesitation, all of the footmen lining the hall filed out into the receiving room. The Emperor's gaze dropped to Garrick's people. "I said leave us."

Garrick gave Malchance and Talon a small nod and he watched as they too quickly left the room.

Once the door had closed securely behind them Groudin reached out and gripped Garrick's forearm. Garrick could see that the familiar look in his father's eyes had returned.

"Garrick, I need your help."

"Help? What is going on Father?"

"Hush and listen. I may not have enough time." The grip on Garrick's arm hardened and the tendons stood out starkly against the back of Groudin's hand. Garrick put a rein on his questions and shut his mouth.

"Son, I love both you and your brother, remember that. Always. Remember that. My mind is not always my own. Something is being done to me and I am powerless to stop it. You need to find out for me and stop it before it can be turned on you. There is magic involved here so tread carefully."

"Any idea as to who is doing this?"

The old man shook his head. "I first thought it to be either Ranen or Felian, but they are

85

not sorcerers."

"There is nothing stopping them from finding one-" Garrick's sentence was cut off as his father's grip abruptly relaxed from his arm and the personality that flashed briefly now retreated from his eyes. They glassed over and his face fell slack.

"Hello my boy, come to see your father? Where is Harada? I haven't seen him in a long while…"

Garrick let his hand drop back into his lap, shocked at the abrupt change that had come over his father.

"Father, we just talked about this. Harada is Hatar Kalar, he cannot come to see you anymore. You will need to go and see him."

"Oh, yes of course…I remember."

It was obvious to Garrick that he didn't.

"Father. I think you need to rest, you are not feeling well," Garrick said as a senior footman entered the room followed by two more servants. The senior footman dropped into a deep bow.

"Is everything to your satisfaction your Imperial Highness?"

The Emperor's eyes perked up at this.

"Yes. Yes, it is."

Garrick turned in his seat and looked hard at the three servants. He did not recognize any of them and they did not have the mark of the Kalar on them.

"I think my father needs to rest," Garrick said as he stood from his chair. "He has over taxed himself."

"Yes Prince Garrick," the man answered still in his bow.

After one last look at his father, Garrick left the room. Malchance and Talon were waiting just outside. He did not stop for them but continued walking out of the receiving room and down the corridor. It wasn't long before Malchance fell into step beside him. It was not until they were back in Garrick's apartments before Garrick flopped into a chair and rubbed the bridge of his nose as he released all his pent up muscles. Malchance took the seat opposite while Talon stayed back by the door.

"What happened?" Malchance asked when it became apparent that Garrick was not going to speak straight away.

Garrick quickly recounted what his father had told him and described the change in demeanor that came over his father as the man talked.

"That is not good Garrick. That means there is an unknown Spellcrafter operating in the Imperial Palace." Malchance jabbed a finger into the arm of his chair for emphasis. "I had a talk with some of the junior footmen after we had been sent out. Most of them have not been in the position long. They told me they are only allowed three months in a position before they are moved to another within the palace."

"She moves them in the hope they don't form a connection to father, and will not become familiar with their routine," Garrick said coming out of his funk.

"Exactly. And for the Spellcrafter to be able to keep a memory spell like what you described going will need to be in constant close contact with your father."

"The senior footman maybe?"

"Maybe. I'm thinking someone more senior to that though. Let me investigate. I'll find out about your father's staff and who they are reporting to. Most of my palace contacts should still be in place."

Garrick shot an eyebrow up at this news.

"Don't look like that Garrick. You wanted me to be your spymaster, what is a better way to practice than to spy on your closest friends."

"I don't care how you gather your information, as long as it helps us to free father and to restore the country's power back to where it belongs."

"Very well Garrick, I'll start putting my feelers out."

"And I am finally going to start exercising

my rights as Crown Prince."

CHAPTER SEVEN

"You can't do this!"

Garrick's internal anger had risen but outwardly he looked as he always had. The authority in his gaze was unmistakable and the Prince now leveled that gaze on his father's chamberlain. Standing with Garrick were Duke

Malchance and several senior ministers.

"I am Crown Prince Garrick Thurad, Right Hand to the Imperial Throne. It is by that that I have the right to do exactly this. My father is unwell and because of this I am evoking an Act of Regency until my father's capacity has been restored."

"Chamberlain Morris, Prince Garrick is correct. His father gave him this authority when he married and it has never been revoked. And by our agreement, he has the government majority necessary to evoke this Regency." Minister Settine said as he stepped forward, planting himself right between Garrick and Morris.

Garrick knew Minister Settine. He knew him very well as they had grown up together, though Settine was a few years older than he. Settine was a supporter of the Royal Family and Garrick knew that he was not comfortable with seeing his Prince argue with an underling.

Malchance took Settine's cue to move forward. "Chamberlain Morris, Prince Garrick has requested that all the palace staff is to assemble in the main courtyard straight away. You will do well to be there to meet them because they will be gathering whether you like it or not. The Prince has already given the order."

"But-"

"There are no buts. You will know the reason for this along with everyone else when Prince Garrick speaks to the staff."

The Chamberlain quickly shut his mouth, looked quickly at the faces of the people around him and just as quickly turned on his heel and left.

"Thank the One he's gone," Garrick muttered.

"We need to do this quickly and seamlessly Garrick," Malchance quickly slipped in. "I have our people ready to go and the servants who are loyal know what is going on."

"I know Willard. I know this has to be done. I'm just dreading the retaliation that we will get. At least I know that whatever happens, father will be safe."

"Yes. Felian needs him alive to be able to keep power."

Noise from numerous people began to rise from outside and Garrick knew that it would not be long now before he starts to set things in motion.

"It's time Prince Garrick," Minister Settine said as one of Garrick's guard opened the door slightly and gave Captain Talon a nod.

"Settine, you can just call me Garrick."

Garrick shook his head. Some things will never change. The man had been calling him that since they were kids.

"Let's get this over with," Garrick muttered and strode across the hall closely followed by Captain Talon and the rest of Garrick's group. Talon had set up his men to form a tight security ring around the courtyard. The man did not want to take any chances that Felian or one of her supporters will try something.

Two of Garrick's guard opened the doors and Garrick stepped out onto the entrance area, striding across the flagstones until he neared the first step, where he stopped. Down in the courtyard, he could see the hundreds of people who worked within the Imperial Palace ranging from the lowliest stable boy to the Palace Chamberlain. Upon seeing him, the crowd fell silent. Garrick placed his hands behind his back and took a deep breath.

"Good morning to you all. For those who are new and do not know me, I am Crown Prince Garrick Thurad." He paused to let that information sink in and to gauge the reaction from the crowd. They remained quiet and to Garrick looked a little fearful.

"As my father is ill, I am evoking my Right to Regency until he has recovered to my physician's satisfaction. My first duty is to assess the staff here at the palace. As of this moment, all palace positions have been revoked. Exceptions to this are staff who have had a request from Duke Malchance to stay on. All other positions will be assessed by the Duke's office and may be reappointed at a later date. I wanted to tell you this personally as I know that for the non-kalar, this may be your only source of income. Because of this, you will be getting a month's pay which will help until you are hired back or have found another position."

"I never received a message," Garrick heard Chamberlain Morris whisper urgently to Malchance.

"Which means you will hear from me when we have assessed your position."

Garrick could not hear Morris's response as the assembled crowd erupted in a cacophony of noise.

"Willard, Settine, Ministers. I think you can take this from here." Garrick then turned on his heel and headed back into the hall. Captain Talon and his men fell in quickly behind him.

"You all need to go to the Pursers office to receive your month's stipend. Messengers will be sent to you when you are able to come back in to work." Garrick heard Malchance say before the doors of the hall closed behind them effectively shutting out the questions from those outside.

"Where to now Prince Garrick," Talon asked.

"We head back to my rooms. I need a drink."

The Captain nodded and Garrick was glad the man was sensible enough not to say anything about what must be a sour look on his face. He did not like doing what he just did. But he agreed with Malchance. It was necessary. It was the only thing they could think of to do quickly that would rid the palace of most of Felian's eyes and ears. The remaining staff was those Garrick knew or were relatives of trusted retainers. But still. What he just did would affect people's livelihoods and it would have lost him support from that area.

Garrick had just finished his first drink when Malchance returned. "I thought you would already be going through the Chamberlain's office Willard," he said raising his now empty glass to the Duke.

"I'm giving the man a chance to pack his personal items under a watchful eye. One he's left, then I am going to go through it all."

"How polite of you."

"It's a damn sight nicer than they would be to us, Garrick."

"True. We would already be locked away downstairs in the dungeons awaiting execution."

Malchance snorted. "I don't think our arses would have even seen the dungeon. We would have been sent straight to the gallows." Malchance sat in the chair next to Garrick and leaned his head against its back. "I know you didn't want to do that Garrick, but it had to be done."

"I know. It is the quickest way of clearing the palace of Felian's spies. At least the ones that are servants." Garrick placed his empty glass on the side table next to him. "The palace guard is going to be a harder nut to crack."

"Not really. We know who we can trust in the guard, and we know who is loyal to the crown. We can replace suspect members of the palace guard with members of your royal guard. At least until those guards can be assessed."

"Felian will not take this calmly Willard. We'd better be ready for the worst that she can throw at us. And it will be me she will come after. With father in her grip, she does not need me to retain power. I hate seeing father like this, it's not right."

"We'll be ready Garrick. Captain Talon and his men will not let anything happen to you."

Garrick smiled as a thought struck him. "For all, I know she probably just poisoned me with that drink I just had."

"Don't be ridiculous. Everything is tested before it even enters your suite."

Garrick leaned forward in his chair and looked first at Talon standing by the door and then at Duke Malchance.

"We have set the first of our pieces on the board. Let us hope that she takes the bait."

CHAPTER EIGHT

I am doing this for father and for the good of the nation. At first, I was too young and stupid to notice, at least Willard had the sense to hide Kalena away. Oh, Caitin my love. Why did you have to go? You would have loved Kalena. And then we sat for years and waited for the right time to act.

We waited too long. Felian's claws have dipped into everything and everything can be linked back to her. She is the disease at the heart of the empire. And like a bloated tumor, she needs to be cut out and burned. It is the only way to save Suene. It is the only way to save the Empire. It is the only way to save Father and Kalena.

Garrick started awake in a cold sweat. The sheets and blankets were twisted about his legs and arms, and a few of his pillows had been knocked to the floor.

He lay still, looking up at the dark canopy over his bed. The dream had been so real. He could still feel the sensation of the last kiss Caitin had given him and the weight of his newborn child in his arms. Tears streamed down his cheeks to soak the silk of his pillowcase. His family was ruined because of that woman! That creature! He dragged his arm across his eyes, wiping away the tears and then used that hand to throw off the tangled blankets.

Garrick dressed quickly and then made his way out to his receiving room where he could already smell breakfast waiting for him. He had barely sat down at his breakfast table when Malchance pounced on him.

"Garrick, you look terrible."

"You don't look too chipper yourself," Garrick shot back with a crooked smile.

Malchance took the chair opposite him and shooed the servants away. They took the hint and left the room, leaving them to talk freely.

"Did you have that dream again?"

Garrick nodded. "It's getting longer too."

"Longer?"

"I spend more time with Caitin before…before…"

"Before Caitin and Kalena leave you."

Garrick nodded.

"It hurts so much Willard. I miss her so much."

Malchance started to reach over to Garrick but stopped himself. "I know Garrick. I know, I miss her too," he said as he settled back into his chair.

"Enough about my dreams."

Garrick took this moment to dig his fork into the small pile of scrambled eggs on his plate and take a mouthful. "You must be here this early in the morning for a reason?"

"Yes, Garrick. You have been invited to

attend the Evening Service at the Cathedral today. As your father is unable to attend, they have requested that you might consider coming in his place."

Garrick took another forkful of his eggs.

"I see no issue with that. It will be good to see the Bishop again and to see how the church has fared in these uncertain times."

"We will have to cross the city at night on our return from the Cathedral. Captain Talon will have a conniption when he learns of this."

Garrick smiled.

"Talon having a conniption? I'd love to witness that."

"Be serious Garrick. It would be the perfect opportunity for someone to make an attempt on your life."

"At least I feel safer eating my breakfast this morning."

Malchance leaned forward as Garrick knew he had hit on the real reason Malchance was here.

"I didn't need to do much digging to find a veritable rat's nest among the servants Felian had in place here. The Chamberlain left a treasure trove of papers and information behind when he left."

"So, I did the right thing with the servants then?"

Malchance nodded. "The servants and public officials control the Royal Palace. If you have control of them, you have control of everything."

Garrick finished off the last of his eggs and took a drink of his coffee. "Talon reported that he did not have much trouble with the Royal Guard."

"No. Over half of them are known to be loyal to you Garrick. The rest have been replaced from your personal guard. Talon did have a few grumblings, but he quickly nipped that in the bud."

"It looks like we have done the impossible and have succeeded in a bloodless takeover."

"As I said Garrick, you need to be careful. Felian is going to push back."

Garrick grinned. "You are beginning to sound just like an old woman Willard. I get it. I understand. And we'll be ready for her. We have been planning this for a very long time, and I don't plan on failure."

Malchance pursed his lips and sat back in his chair.

"Don't look at me like that. I know you are a habitual worrywart, but you need to relax. At least for a moment."

"Very well, I'll let you finish your breakfast in peace. I'll be in the Chamberlain's office today if you need me, tidying up the headache he left for me. I'll be back to get you for the service this evening."

"Yes mother," Garrick replied, a crooked smile on his face.

"I've been managing your time for a decade, I'm not about to stop now."

"And I wouldn't want you to."

Malchance rose from his seat and gave Garrick a light bow. "Your Highness."

"Your Grace."

And with that Malchance left to let Garrick eat in peace.

Shatal bared his teeth and took a nip at Malchance's grey.

"I think Shatal has a thing against greys. He took a dislike to High Provost Deten's grey as well, "Garrick said as he reined the horse's head back.

It was evening. The Service had been quick and the sermon short. But the populous had seen him in his father's place, in his father's seat which is what Bishop Tomas had intended.

Outside, the streets were still crowded with people rushing about their business, though a good many of them wore the robes of the clergy.

Garrick moved Shatal closer to Malchance to get out of the way of the human traffic.

"I knew we should not have come out for this. Look at the people, and they are all watching us."

Garrick chose to ignore Malchance. His resolution to be nice to him had nearly dwindled away with all his moaning if he mentions assassination one more time though...

"They are here to see me most likely, word has passed around that I was at the service tonight." His voice was stiff and unemotional.

Malchance nodded, his eyes now constantly scanning those in the crowd around them, his left hand casually gripping his sword hilt. They made their way towards the end of the busy road. Lost in thought, Garrick moved his horse through the press of the crowd, barely feeling Malchance's presence next to him.

Suddenly, the buildings beside him fell away and the two of them was standing at a large, well paved intersection. Wooden signs swinging gently on metal arms proclaimed the names of the streets that met at the corner. They had just come down a street called Chapel Street that entered onto a large thoroughfare simply called The Academy. Looking across the wide boulevard, Garrick could see the elegant form of a building rising over the heads of the river of people.

"Wasn't Talan and his men meeting us here?" Garrick asked.

Malchance started to nod and stopped. He sat his horse stock-still and then his left hand slowly tightened its grip on his sword hilt.

"What is it, Willard?" Garrick looked at the warrior and then tried to peer across the road, his height not being as great as Malchance's putting him at a disadvantage.

"I cannot see anything," Garrick said crossly to himself.

"There's something not right here. I think we'd best go back down the street and wait," Malchance muttered.

Both men turned their horses and moved back around the corner into Chapel Street. The noise of the crowd drowning their talk to just themselves. Looking constantly around him, Malchance's worry and fear began to make Garrick uneasy.

"Malchance, what is going on?" he demanded once they were far enough down the street.

"There were members of Felian's paid

network waiting outside that building for you to pass. I cannot let them see you." He said the last more to himself.

"Let them see me. What have I to fear from citizens that report what they see? Hundreds have seen me already in the last few minutes. What would five or six more hurt?"

"Remember, I am here to protect you." He then looked back in the direction of the thoroughfare, watching for any sign that they were being followed. "We'd best dismount as we wait for Talon. I don't want us to be bigger targets than we have to be."

Garrick grudgingly nodded agreement and quickly dismounted, being careful to avoid kicking anyone in the crowd around them. "You don't really think that Felian's henchmen will try anything with all these people around do you?"

"It pays to be careful Garrick. It is easier to kill someone unawares in a crowd than in an empty room."

Garrick looked about him and saw the wisdom in Malchance's words. The moving crowd made the perfect cover for anyone up to no good. He now began to feel guilty about his earlier thoughts about the Duke. "I now regret asking Talon to meet up with us here because I want to be up close with my people."

Suddenly familiar faces came strolling through the crowd from the direction of The Cathedral. Garrick quickly jabbed a finger in their direction. "There is Talon and the Guard."

Malchance turned in the direction of Garrick's finger and nodded to himself.

"Come on."

Slowly, they began to push their way through the crowd towards the small group of armored men. Their towering height made it easy to see them through the press of people and they seemed to move forward in the crowd like the prow of a boat cutting through the water. Swords and shields acting as a deterrent to the uncaring pushing crowd.

"Hail, Prince Garrick!" A voice called somewhere in the crowd. Garrick cursed under his breath.

Captain Talon stopped his men on spotting them rushing towards him through the crowd. His sudden halt stunned those people swarming around him into a momentary standstill.

A soft whistling sound sped past Garrick's

ear and the woman in front of him silently crumpled to the ground, a splash of red showing the feathered dart which hit her.

Another whistled through the empty air where his shoulder was as Malchance pulled him quickly towards the Soldiers, hitting another bystander. Garrick watched helplessly as the man's eyes rolled up and he slumped silently to the ground.

Around them, the stilled mass of people began to scream and run wildly from the street as they began to realize what was going on around them.

Releasing the reins of the horses, Malchance pulled Garrick roughly to him and enclosed him in a tight bear hug, turning his back to the direction in which the darts were coming.

"Talon, help us get to cover!" Garrick shouted over the screaming of the stampeding crowd.

Captain Talon and his men were already heading in their direction, fighting against the crush of people trying to escape from the street.

People trying to escape the danger were buffeting Malchance from all sides. Garrick could feel the shove of every person that came in contact with him though Malchance did his best to protect him from that as well.

Suddenly the sound of the fleeing crowds was gone, replaced by that of the Prince's Guard who formed a protective box around them. Malchance quickly released Garrick from his arms and quickly drew his sword with one smooth motion to hold it glinting in the evening light.

Garrick stepped back away from the sword and came up hard against Captain Talon. Before him was the man who had fallen, his body trampled by the crowds in the rush to get away. Lying just outside the circle of men was the crumpled body of the woman.

"It seems that trouble has followed you." Captain Talon said with a frown across his bare face, his sword held comfortably across his right shoulder. Around them, Garrick's heavily armed and armored bodyguard stood with weapons raised waiting. The Captain had not been happy about the change in orders when they left the Cathedral.

"This is no time to dispute your orders Captain," Garrick growled, drawing his sword.

"Well," Talon said as he looked full circle around at the seemingly empty buildings that faced onto the vacated street. "It seems that your playmates have gone."

Garrick did not answer him, he stood with his sword before him and waited.

Minutes passed and Garrick glanced uncertainly at the buildings around him. Sweat beaded on his brow and he nervously wiped it away with the sleeve of his coat. Everything was now silent in the street, only the occasional creak of leather and metal from the Guard making any noise.

Then slowly figures began to appear from the buildings around them. They seemed to pull themselves from the very cracks in the roof tile, seeping out from the shadows of stone walls and small alleyways. They approached the circle slowly.

Around their circle stood six men. Garrick

could see the line of Malchance's jaw tighten as he saw the emblems that they wore openly on their black cloaks. Embroidered in a scarlet thread was an open book surrounded by a circle. A corrupted symbol of the Justicars.

Looking at the men, in turn, Garrick could distinguish no difference in appearance between them. They all had dark hair, dark eyes, pale skin and were the same height. They stood staring at them, unmoving. Garrick, Malchance and the guard stared silently back.

Suddenly, as if to a silent cue, the six drew swords and charged into the circle of guards. In the blink of an eye, one of Talon's men crashed to the ground in a spray of blood. A black cloaked figure came to stand over the body, the serrated edge of his sword gleamed red as it caught the light.

Malchance moved himself to stand between the figure and Garrick. Garrick felt Talon move suddenly away from him. Turning he saw the Captain catch a wicked edged sword on the crosspiece of his blade before aiming a solid punch at the man's jaw. The Dark Justicar fell to the ground and Talon stepped forward to fill the spot of another of his fallen men.

Garrick now stood by himself in the center of the whirling circle of blades. He spun around at the sound of every loud grunt or cry, thinking that another Dark Justicar had broken through the line of men to attack him.

Malchance still stood facing the first Dark Justicar who had now moved passed the body before him without giving it a second glance.

The man's face wore an unnatural grin, lips

125

peeled back to reveal tightly clenched yellow teeth.

His eyes were opened as wide as his lids allowed showing more white than iris, he looked as if he was in terrible agony. But he moved not like a man in pain but with the grace of a wild cat.

Malchance was now crouched in a fighter's stance, his sword held at an angle before him. The Dark Justicar stopped his approach just out of lunging range and stood to smile his hideous, rictus smile. His unnatural gaze moved slowly from Malchance's face to rest eagerly on Garrick. His skin seemed to crawl under that gaze and he felt the need to scratch himself all over.

A flash of light caught his eye and saw the man lurch backward.

Embedded to the hilt in his shoulder was one of Malchance's daggers. Another dagger was now balanced in Malchance's left-hand waiting.

"Take your eyes off him."

Slowly, the man grasped the dagger and pulled it from his flesh. He glanced fleetingly at the dagger before tossing it to the cobblestones.

Garrick stood as still as stone, watching every move the man made. All around them the Guard was still fighting, though two more were missing from their numbers. There was only one more black cloaked body to add to the enemy dead.

"You have no hope of winning," Garrick simply said

"We were just asked to deliver a message, My Prince if we could not kill you," the man said conversationally.

Garrick grunted to himself before replying. "What message do have for me then." Shouts could now be heard coming from the end of Chapel Street. Garrick looked behind him to see a group of heavily armed Temple Warriors coming towards them from The Academy.

"I have a message to deliver to you. I am to tell you that there is no place where you are safe, that there is no place where you can hide, that eventually you will bow to my Mistress and everything you have will be hers. She would prefer it to be willing. If not," the man shrugged.

Suddenly the man began to laugh insanely. The others who accompanied him were hacked down by Talon and his men as they too began to laugh. His laughter quickly turned to a gurgling noise and the man began to claw frantically at his throat. Garrick watched in horror as blood began to flow freely from his nose, eyes, and mouth. He slowly sank to the ground as his legs crumpled beneath him.

Malchance walked forward and nudged him hard with the toe of his boot. The Dark Justicar did not stir.

"He is dead," pronounced Malchance as Temple Warriors came to join them.

The Commander of the Temple Warriors gave them an irritated look. "What is going on here?" The woman asked as both Duke Malchance and Captain Talon approached her. The Commander's gaze skimmed quickly over the many bodies that now lay across Chapel Street. Her eyes widened as she saw the emblem on the black cloaks of the dead.

"We have had some trouble," Captain Talon said.

"More than you realize." Garrick sheathed his sword and approached the small group and they slowly began to explain what had happened to the Temple Commander.

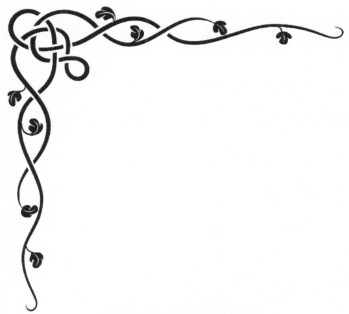

CHAPTER NINE

"Garrick, you have to act now."

Malchance had followed hot on Garrick's heels and spoke as soon as Captain Talon closed the door to his receiving rooms.

"You can't let this go without repercussions. They tried to kill you, Garrick.

Treason was committed. You must make an example of them."

"I must? The word 'must' is not used to princes." Garrick rounded on Malchance, using him to expel the pent up fear and adrenaline that he had been keeping contained in that one sentence. It would not do to show any weakness in public. Not now.

Garrick released the breath he was holding. "But, a prince should never flinch from doing acts of ruthlessness which are necessary for safeguarding the State and their own person."

Talon suddenly straightened as if about to accept orders and Malchance's look of fury quickly evaporated into one of quiet expectation.

"A prince must take these things so much to heart that they do not fear to strike even the very

132

nearest that you have if they are implicated."

The words were from a treatise on rulership that his Great Grandfather had written for his son, and that book had been memorized by every royal child since then. But only now did Garrick truly understand what that phrase really meant.

Garrick looked at his childhood friend, his shield and protector. He was acutely aware that their torn and dirty clothes also carried the blood of innocent victims caught between Felian and her bid for power. He had let this go on long enough. The innocent should not pay in blood for his squeamish conscience.

"Find Ranen and Felian, and those who harbor them. They are to be held under arrest for committing High Treason."

"By your order Prince Garrick." Malchance

snapped his heels together and quickly strode from the room followed by Talon.

"Right, search every room!" Captain Talon stood in the atrium to the Great Hall of Ranen's home, staring grimly at his men as they began to fan out through the rest of the house. "You two, upstairs," Talon jabbed a finger at two men still loitering in the hall and then pointed up to the main staircase.

Malchance stood off to one side next to Ranen's wife and two children, flanked by two of Garrick's guardsmen, watching.

"My husband is not here. He left early this

afternoon and has not returned."

"Do you know where he was going?"

"No, sir." The woman hugged her children closer as the sounds of booted feet began to be heard in all areas of the building.

Malchance smiled at the woman. "You have beautiful, well behaved children."

"Thank you Duke Malchance."

"I wish I had a daughter. Girls can bring such joy to a family, can't they? Do you mind?" Malchance held his hands out to the little girl who looked to be no more than maybe three or four. The woman hesitated and he saw the grip around the child's shoulder tighten before the women reluctantly let her arm slip away.

Malchance reached down and lifted the little girl into his arms. "What pretty hair you have. What is your name?"

The little girl smiled at the compliment and ran a pudgy hand over her blonde curls. "My name is Raynar."

"It's very nice to meet you, Raynor." Malchance smiled down at the girl. Her mother anxiously watched them both. Malchance ignored the woman. He stepped a short distance away from them, turning so that the little girl's back was to her mother. "Do you know where your father is?" The little girl shook her head, but her eyes automatically moved to the dark wood paneling to the right of the fireplace. He slowly placed the little girl back on the floor and her mother quickly reached forward and snatched her close.

"Captain Talon?"

"Sir."

Malchance moved to the wall and studied the intricately carved wood. The same woodland vine motif was echoed across all the panels, all fresh and new. Except for one. A panel carving to the far right shared the same motif, but it was dull, the polish had been worn away. Especially around that thick carved flower. The Duke reached out and touched a finger to the hard, wood petals and heard a feminine gasp come from behind him. He smiled.

He gripped the flower and twisted. A soft click was heard behind the wood and a large section of the wood paneling opened an inch away from the rest of the wall. Malchance nodded to Talon who pulled the door fully open to reveal a small room, dimly lit by a small smokeless lantern and huddled in black wool robes in the far corner was the pudgy form of Ranen.

The next morning, Garrick was reading through the documents that Malchance had handed him. The first of which was the charges laid out for treason and attempted murder. Then on the next several pages was all the evidence they had collected to show these charges be true and accurate, and then, on the final page was a very long list of names. A list of names much longer than what Garrick thought it should be.

"For a Justicar, Ranen quickly turned on his allies and fellow conspirators." Garrick spread the papers across his work desk.

"Yes, he did. We had not even started the

138

interrogation before he started spilling names, schemes and murder plots."

"I thought they were supposed to be made of firmer stuff than that."

"You would think so. Ranen must have gotten used to soft living as the High Justicar. Plus he has a wife and two children. His cooperation will ensure that they are not stripped of their money or rank."

Garrick nodded and picked up the last page from his table. Ranen and Felian's names were at the top of that list, but as his eyes moved down, he saw several names that surprised him at being there.

"Are you sure of these?" Garrick asked holding the list up for Malchance to see.

"Yes. Names I was not sure of are on another list in my office awaiting further investigation."

Garrick released the page and let it flutter down on his desk and stepped back to the charge sheet. At the bottom of that page was a large space awaiting his signature and Seal. Garrick sighed and flicked open his inkwell and picked up his pen.

"Arrest them all Willard. And let it all be done."

The decision had been made. Dipping his pen in the inkwell, Garrick quickly signed his name to the bottom of the document. Malchance dobbed melted wax from the heated wax stick at the signatures' end and Garrick lifted his Great Seal from its box and stamped it into the cooling blob.

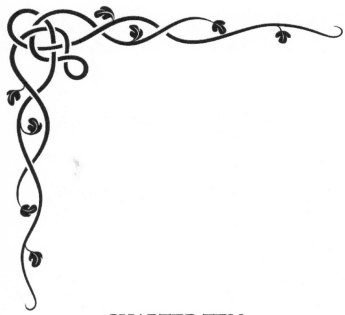

CHAPTER TEN

"Felian has escaped us. And the man that we had under watch as her suspected spellcrafter, the senior footman, has disappeared as well."

Talon stood just inside the door of the seneschal's office, which was now Duke Malchance's office. The Duke was seated at the work desk shuffling papers and Garrick stood to one side looking through the small glazed window to the courtyard down below.

"Have the city searched for them. Increase the scrutiny at the city gates for people, animals and vehicles entering and leaving Hered."

"Yes, Prince Garrick." Captain Talon bowed his head. "Are there any other orders?"

"The Emperor is not to be disturbed. The Physician says that he is in desperate need of rest and recuperation if he is to recover completely from his ensnarement. Duke Malchance and I are the only visitors that can see him. All food, drink and medicines are to be thoroughly vetted before going into his presence."

"Yes, your highness." Talon bowed again and took a step back before he turned and strode for the door.

Once the door was closed Garrick looked to Malchance. "Were Felian and her pet magic user the only ones to escape?"

Malchance shook his head. "Two Justicars on the arrest list have not yet been found either. Felian has not been seen since yesterday evening. I suspect that as soon as she heard of the failure of the assassination, she left the city. I do not think we will find her here."

"She would not have gone far though. That woman does not like to be too far away from power."

"She also values her skin remaining unblemished and keeping her head attached to her neck Garrick, the woman will not stay around here."

Garrick poured himself a drink from the

crystal decanter the Duke kept by the window, he turned and offered Malchance to refill the glass he had but the Duke waved it away accompanied with a shake of his head.

"She will not get far," Garrick said after taking a drink from his glass and looking back out of the window. "The empire will be hunting for her and anyone who aids her. She tried to kill me and I still believe that she was behind Caitin's death. It is because of her that my daughter grew up without knowing who her parents are and is now a Hatar Kalar."

A loud screech sounded through the room making Garrick wince as it grated against his eardrums. It came from outside, heard even through the thick stone walls of the palace and a large shadow passed over the ground of the courtyard outside. Guards and servants scurried for cover as a large blue Hatar'le'margarten appeared, back winging to slow its descent onto the now deserted cobblestones.

"What's happened?" Malchance asked as he rushed from his desk to the window.

"A Hatar landing in the courtyard."

Both men watched as the creature set down daintily on all fours and then crouched down on its front legs. The flyer quickly released himself from the flight harness and dismounted from the Hatar as the new Palace Guard rushed out to meet him.

"Do you recognize them?" Malchance asked.

"I do, they are from Harada's Flight, though I can't remember their names."

As the two men watched the scene from the

window, after a brief discussion, the small group of the guard and the Hatar Kalar now moved in their direction.

"He's here to see you, Garrick. That can only mean Harada or Oded has some bad news for us."

"Let's hope to the One that it's only that the Arranian's have attacked."

Placing his glass back by the decanter, Garrick quickly left the room to meet with the Hatar Kalar.

To Be Continued in

Part 10

The Gathering

Thank you so much for reading and I hope to see you again.

Thank you for reading my book. If you enjoyed it, won't you please take a moment to leave me a review?

THE KALARTHRI

The Way to Freedom, Book One

"This Hatar Kalar has more natural Talent than any Second Born found in the Empire."

Every ten years the Imperium Provosts travel the provinces of the Great Suene Empire and take every second born child as the property of the Emperor. His Due for their continued protection.

Kalena, taken from her family and friends finds herself alone and scared in the imperial Stronghold of Darkon. And when she cries out to the darkness for help, Kalena is shocked when it answers her back.

If you found out that you were different from everyone else, what would you do?

HOWLING VENGEANCE

John McCall Mysteries, Book One

John McCall just wanted to get a surprise for his men. Instead he got a disemboweled body.

A man is arrested for the murder but McCall is sure that they have the wrong person.

And when McCall starts digging around for the truth, he unearths a whole lot more than he bargained for.

Howling Vengeance. A supernatural mystery in the Old West.

Available now at your favorite Online Bookseller

THE ENCLAVE

The Verge, Book One

Katherine Kirk lived only for vengeance.

Vengeance against the man who destroyed her home, her family and her life.

Sent on a babysitting mission to Junter 3, RAN officer Katherine Kirk, finds herself quickly embroiled in the politics between the New Holland Government and the Val Myran refugees claiming asylum.

After an Alliance attack Kirk and her team hunt the enemy down and discover that they have finally found the lair of the man they have been searching for…

And the captive who has been waiting patiently for rescue.

"What would you do to the man who destroyed every important person in your life?"

Winter's Magic

Book One of The Order

Kaitlyn Winter is biting at the bit to become an active agent for the Restricted Practitioners Unit. And on her first day in the job she is thrown into a virtual s**t storm (to put it nicely).

First, she gets targeted for Assassination by The Sharda's top assassin

Second, her Werewolf best friend decides that her being '*Straight*' means she can't protect herself and places her in protective custody

Third, the love of her life still won't notice her existence and the Tempus Mage who's set to keep an eye on her is infuriatingly attractive….

You can find out more information and sign up for Hayley's monthly newsletter on her website
http://www.hmclarkeauthor.com/

Proven
Book one of The Blackwatch Chronicles

Something is rotten in the city of Brookhaven. And it is up to the Blackwatch to root it out.

All Ryn Weaver ever wanted was to be a warrior. To protect others unable to protect themselves. But on her Proving to join the prestigious Blackwatch Order she finds herself accidentally Paired with Dagan Drake, a Tribunal Mage. Theirs is a reluctant partnership. Given no choice in the matter, Ryn must now work with Dagan to complete his mission to capture a traitor to the realm.

With rogue mages and brutish blades coming at her from every turn, will Ryn be able to gain the respect of her new partner and prove herself worthy of her blade? Or will Ryn and her Order fall to the machinations of the evil set against them?

Proven is the first installment in a new epic fantasy romance series. If you like electrifying action, rich characters, and magical battles, then you'll love H.M. Clarke's series starter. Click to read Proven now.

ABOUT THE AUTHOR

In a former life, H M Clarke has been a Console Operator, an ICT Project Manager, Public Servant, Paper Shuffler and an Accountant (the last being the most exciting.)

She attended Flinders University in Adelaide, South Australia, where she studied for a Bachelor of Science (Chem), and also picked up a Diploma in Project Management while working for the South Australian Department of Justice.

In her spare time, she likes to lay on the couch and watch TV, garden, draw, read, and tell ALL her family what wonderful human beings they are.

She keeps threatening to go out and get a real job (Cheesecake Test Taster sounds good) and intends to retire somewhere warm and dry – like the middle of the Simpson Desert. For the time being however, she lives in Ohio and dreams about being warm…

You can find out more information and sign up for Hayley's monthly newsletter on her website –
http://hmclarkeauthor.com
http://eepurl.com/SPy61

Or catch her on Twitter - **@hmclarkeauthor**

Made in the USA
Las Vegas, NV
28 February 2021

18779014R00100